HAWKS

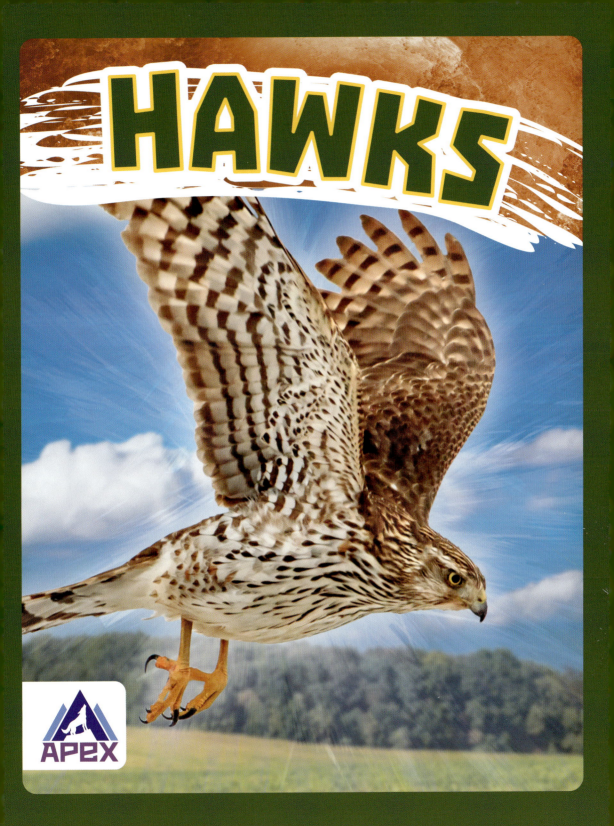

BY MEGAN GENDELL

WWW.APEXEDITIONS.COM

Copyright © 2022 by Apex Editions, Mendota Heights, MN 55120. All rights reserved. No part of this book may be reproduced or utilized in any form or by any means without written permission from the publisher.

Apex is distributed by North Star Editions:
sales@northstareditions.com | 888-417-0195

Produced for Apex by Red Line Editorial.

Photographs ©: Shutterstock Images, cover (bird), 1 (bird), 4–5, 6–7, 8–9, 10–11, 12, 13, 14–15, 16–17, 18–19, 20, 21, 22–23, 24, 25, 26–27, 29; Unsplash, cover (background), 1 (background)

Library of Congress Control Number: 2021915668

ISBN
978-1-63738-144-1 (hardcover)
978-1-63738-180-9 (paperback)
978-1-63738-251-6 (ebook pdf)
978-1-63738-216-5 (hosted ebook)

Printed in the United States of America
Mankato, MN
012022

NOTE TO PARENTS AND EDUCATORS

Apex books are designed to build literacy skills in striving readers. Exciting, high-interest content attracts and holds readers' attention. The text is carefully leveled to allow students to achieve success quickly. Additional features, such as bolded glossary words for difficult terms, help build comprehension.

TABLE OF CONTENTS

CHAPTER 1
CATCHING A MEAL 5

CHAPTER 2
BORN TO FLY 11

CHAPTER 3
ON THE HUNT 17

CHAPTER 4
LIFE IN THE WILD 23

Comprehension Questions • 28

Glossary • 30

To Learn More • 31

About the Author • 31

Index • 32

CHAPTER 1
CATCHING A MEAL

A hawk sits on the branch of a tall tree. Suddenly, a mouse runs across the field below. The hawk swoops down to catch it.

A red-tailed hawk can see a mouse from 100 feet (30 m) away.

A hawk has four talons on each foot. One talon faces backward. This talon is extra long and extra sharp.

As the hawk nears the ground, she stretches her legs. She grabs the mouse in her sharp **talons**.

HOLDING ON TIGHT

A hawk's talons have a strong, tight grip. They keep **prey** from escaping. Hawks use their talons to grasp tree branches, too. They hold on tightly even while they sleep.

The hawk carries the mouse back to the tree. She tears pieces of meat with her sharp beak.

A hawk's beak curves down at the end. This hooked shape helps the hawk rip meat.

Red-tailed hawks fly up into trees with small prey. But they stay on the ground to eat bigger prey.

CHAPTER 2

BORN TO FLY

There are dozens of different types of hawks. They come in many colors and sizes. All hawks have good **vision**, hooked beaks, and strong feet.

The gray hawk is known for the stripes, called bars, on its tail feathers.

The ferruginous hawk is the biggest hawk. Its wings can be up to 5 feet (1.5 m) across.

Ferruginous hawks live in grasslands and other open areas.

The rough-legged hawk lives in cold, northern areas around the world.

Large hawks **soar** high in the open air. Long wings help them float in the wind.

SNOW PANTS

The rough-legged hawk lives in very cold places. Its legs are covered in long feathers. These feathers help the bird stay warm.

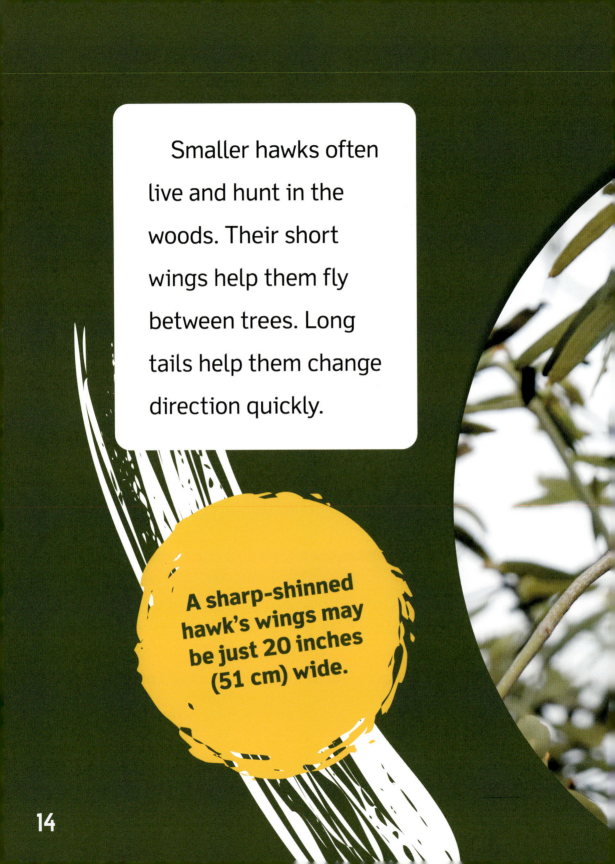

Smaller hawks often live and hunt in the woods. Their short wings help them fly between trees. Long tails help them change direction quickly.

A sharp-shinned hawk's wings may be just 20 inches (51 cm) wide.

The sharp-shinned hawk is the smallest hawk in North America.

CHAPTER 3

ON THE HUNT

Hawks are **predators**. They hunt small animals. They often eat mice, squirrels, and small birds.

Gray-lined hawks often eat lizards, snakes, and frogs.

17

Hawks can't move their eyes. To look around, a hawk must turn its whole head.

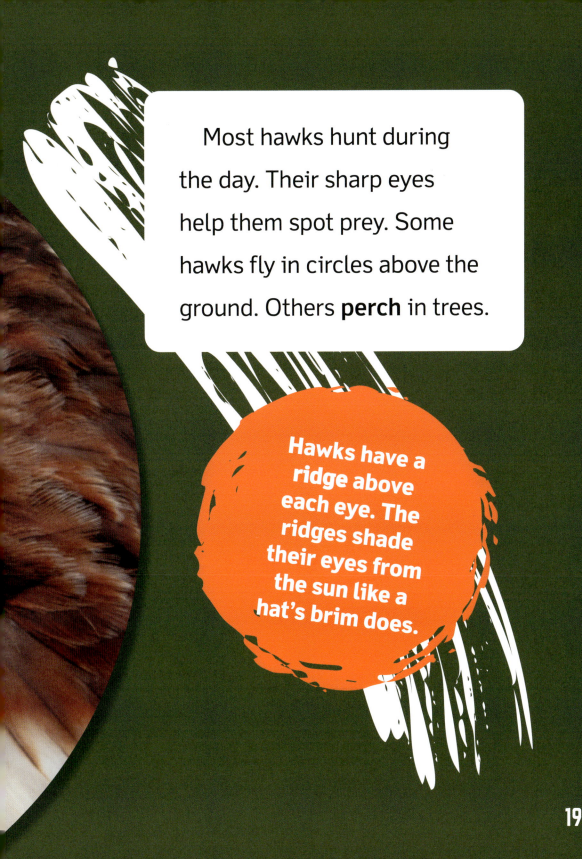

Most hawks hunt during the day. Their sharp eyes help them spot prey. Some hawks fly in circles above the ground. Others **perch** in trees.

Hawks have a ridge above each eye. The ridges shade their eyes from the sun like a hat's brim does.

A red-tailed hawk can dive faster than 120 miles per hour (193 km/h).

When hawks see prey, they dive to catch it. Smaller hawks may chase prey through the woods.

Harris's hawks often gather on branches before working together to hunt prey.

TEAMING UP

Most hawks hunt alone. But Harris's hawks work together. This way, they can catch bigger animals. For example, they can catch a **jackrabbit** that is three times as heavy as one Harris's hawk.

CHAPTER 4
LIFE IN THE WILD

Hawks are found all over the world. Most live in forests or near trees. Some live in deserts or grassy, open areas.

Cooper's hawks tend to live near forests or mountains.

Hawks use sticks to build their nests. They may also gather leaves, bark, or moss.

Hawks build nests in the spring. The female hawk lays eggs. She sits on the eggs to keep them warm and safe.

Most hawks stay with the same mate for their whole lives.

Hawks often build nests in trees or other high places.

After about a month, the eggs hatch. The baby hawks stay in the nest for several weeks. Then they go live on their own.

A female hawk lays up to five eggs each year.

HOME SWEET HOME

Ferruginous hawks use the same nest over and over. They add more sticks each year. Over time, the nest can grow more than 3 feet (1 m) tall.

COMPREHENSION QUESTIONS

Write your answers on a separate piece of paper.

1. Write a few sentences describing the life cycle of a hawk.

2. If you were a hawk, would you rather hunt alone or in a group?

3. What body part helps a hawk tear meat from its prey?

    A. its strong talons
    B. its long wings
    C. its sharp beak

4. How would sitting on eggs help a mother hawk keep them warm?

    A. Heat from the mother hawk's body would go to the eggs.
    B. Heat from the eggs would go to the mother hawk's body.
    C. Heat from the air could not reach the eggs.

5. What does **grasp** mean in this book?

*Hawks use their talons to **grasp** tree branches, too. They hold on tightly even while they sleep.*

    A. let go of
    B. hold on to
    C. tear apart

6. What does **escaping** mean in this book?

*A hawk's talons have a strong, tight grip. They keep prey from **escaping**.*

    A. changing shape
    B. staying still
    C. getting away

Answer key on page 32.

GLOSSARY

jackrabbit
A type of hare. Hares are animals that look similar to rabbits but are bigger.

mate
One of a pair of animals that come together to have babies.

perch
To rest in a high place, such as the branch of a tree.

predators
Animals that hunt and eat other animals.

prey
An animal that is hunted and eaten by another animal.

ridge
A raised strip or bump that sticks up from the area around it.

soar
To fly high in the air without flapping wings very often.

talons
Long, sharp claws that birds use to hunt.

vision
The sense of sight.

TO LEARN MORE

BOOKS

Hamilton, S. L. *Hawks*. Minneapolis: Abdo Publishing, 2018.

Morlock, Theresa. *Red-Tailed Hawk vs. Burmese Python*. New York: Gareth Stevens Publishing, 2019.

Sommer, Nathan. *Hawks*. Minneapolis: Bellwether Media, 2019.

ONLINE RESOURCES

Visit **www.apexeditions.com** to find links and resources related to this title.

ABOUT THE AUTHOR

Megan Gendell is a writer and editor. She lives in Vermont. She likes to take long walks and watch hawks fly above mountaintops.

INDEX

B
beaks, 8, 11

D
deserts, 23

E
eggs, 24, 26
eyes, 19

F
feathers, 13
ferruginous hawk, 12, 27
forests, 23

H
Harris's hawks, 21
hunting, 14, 17, 19, 21

N
nests, 24, 26–27

P
prey, 7, 19–20

R
rough-legged hawk, 13

S
sharp-shinned hawk, 14
soaring, 13

T
tails, 14
talons, 7
trees, 5, 7–8, 14, 19, 23

W
wings, 12–14
woods, 14, 20

Answer Key:
1. Answers will vary; **2.** Answers will vary; **3.** C; **4.** A; **5.** B; **6.** C